ALMA'S
MATTERS

Written by
Ido Weinberg

·

Illustrated by
Ofri Rieger

What's your name?
How old are you?
My name is Alma,
I am two.

I said to Evy, my friend who's three,
two is nice, but not for me...
The games you play, the things you see,
are so much better when you're three!

And Evy said that three is fine,
but four is better any time.
The games you play, the things you see,
at four are better than at three!

When we meet a neighbor or friend,
they always ask how baby is doing...
Even though he can't do anything...
And I can!

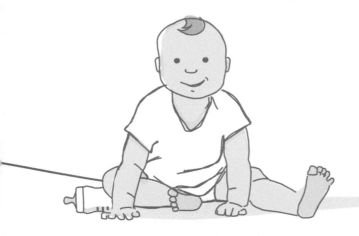

Once I put on a costume, I can pretend,
to be a red dragon, or a little brown hen.
With my wings and a wand, I'm a fairy no less.
With a quick change of clothes, I can be a princess.

Green pants and a 'ribbit' - I'm a frog hopping by;
and once I stop hopping I can change to a fly!
I can be a brave lion, or a wee little mouse.
I can wear a big crown, and be queen of the house!

Yes! I love all my costumes, and it makes me feel great,
to dress up and become all those things that I ain't...

If I wear Daddy's tie, and try on his shoes,
I can be big like he is whenever I choose.
I look in the mirror and love what I see,
and when playtime is over, I change back to me...

When Daddy asks me questions,
he acts like it's okay...
If I know or don't the answers,
he'll love me anyway...

So why is it that when I'm wrong,
he just says "Don't worry. It's okay.",
but if I get the answer right,
he brags and brags all day?!

I like books at bedtime. I like books at dawn.
I like books that are short. I like books that are long.

I like books that are funny, those make me laugh.
I like books with my mommy. I like books with my dad.

I like books with pictures that tell me the stories
of dragons, of wolves and of bears and of bunnies.

I like the one with the monsters and the one with the cat.
I like the book with the tree that I think is quite sad.

I like all my books. Yes! That I do!
I like them alone. I like them in twos.

I like to read books, that's so plain to see.
But I still can't read them, so please read to me!

For my birthday,
I wanted to say:
"Toys are okay,
but a box makes my day!"

When I see a friend I like,
I don't know what to say.
How do I make them like me?
How do we start to play?

I'm going to a new school.
I'll meet some new friends.
And learn how to read...
My time here now ends...

I'll have some new teachers.
I'll tell them my name.
Just tell me please Daddy,
will they love me the same?

In the elevator,
when no-one else will know...
Daddy let's me press the buttons,
of floors above our own...

I get really excited to go on the train,
even if only for one stop,
just to get out of the rain.

The aquarium was fun. They had so many fish to see.
Like goldfish, and green fish and grey fish from the sea.
They also had turtles, crabs, seals and some penguins.
Dad was quick to catch me when I almost swam with em'...

Yes. The aquarium was fun, and I'll have stories to tell:
Of sharks, eels and shells. Of rays with long tails...
When we got home that night, dad said it was truly a win,
because of the great time we've had, and 'cause I never fell in!

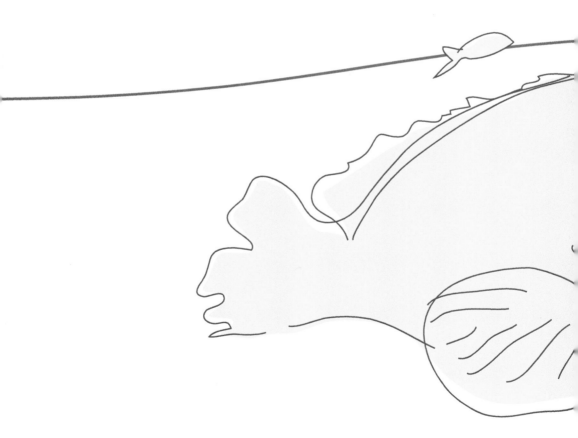

No matter where it is we're going,
being in a car is boring.
There's simply nothing you can do,
to make me like this ride with you!

No. I don't want your games or snacks.
I'm done with sitting in the back.
No more rides for me. I'm done.
Unless I drive... That seems like fun...

I went to a farm
with my dad and my mom.
They had ducks that quacked,
a barbecue shack,
corn on a cob,
chickens and dogs.
They had horses that neighed, and also some sheep.
I counted them all and fell right asleep!

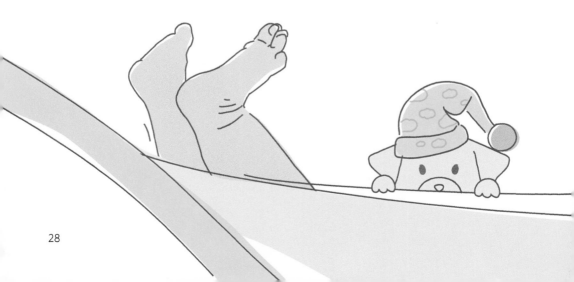

Elevators, buses and other small spaces,
are all filled with strangers with really strange faces.
They all seem so big. They make me feel small.
And some of them stare. I don't like that at all.

But lucky for me, dad's legs are right there.
I can hide right behind them, so those strangers can't stare.
Dad's legs are real long. They're as big as two trees.
From behind Daddy's legs, you can see, but aren't seen.

If I could pick another nose,
I would pick one that is big.
In a nose like that, it is easier to dig...

I love to chase bubbles,
and to pop them one by one,
so please blow bubbles Daddy,
let's have some bubbly fun.

Now let me blow the bubbles,
I can do it on my own.
The nicest bubbles Daddy,
are the ones that I have blown.

Oops. I dropped the bottle.
Now all the soap is gone.
There are no more bubbles Daddy.
Our bubbly fun is done...

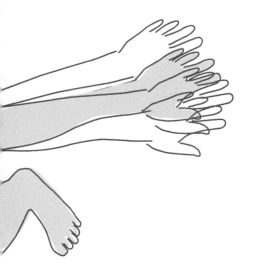

I went to the pool
one hot summer day.
The water was cool,
so I swam and I played.

I kicked and I splashed.
It was lots of fun.
But then I threw up,
and the swimming was done...

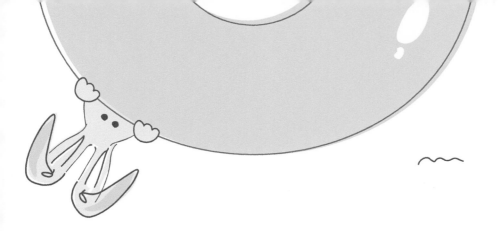

I got burnt from the sun.
Walking on shells wasn't fun.
Cold waves got me wet,
and I still broke out in a sweat.

Seagulls ate my lunch.
Jellyfish sting and I stepped on a bunch.
Sand got in my hair.
There was salt everywhere.

That day at the beach,
was as good as can be!
What could be better,
than a day by the sea?

I wanted some ice-cream, I wanted it so.
When I got some from Mommy I wouldn't let go.
It finally melted and fell on the floor.
If I stop crying, will you get me some more?

I can smell
when you sneak a cookie
under your breath!

My cousins were here
with their mom and their dad.
They stayed for a week
filled with fun that we had.

We slept in a tent.
We went on some trips.
I shared all my stuff.
They bought me some gifts.

We played with my toys,
and we played hide and seek.
We had a great time,
in that way too short week.

We had so much fun,
my three cousins and I.
But then they were gone,
and I started to cry...

I love my brother,
I love him so.
I'll grab his hand,
I won't let go.

I love my brother.
He's on the bed.
I'll jump up too...
Right by his head...

I love my brother.
I don't know why,
I had to scream,
and make him cry...

I love my brother,
but it's not fair!
They love him now,
like I'm thin air...

Every shower night or day,
I lift my chin up in a way,
to keep the soap far from my eyes;
that can be hard, but I sure try...

Then just like clockwork every day,
I put my head down anyway...
The soap comes burning in my eyes,
and that is when I start to cry...

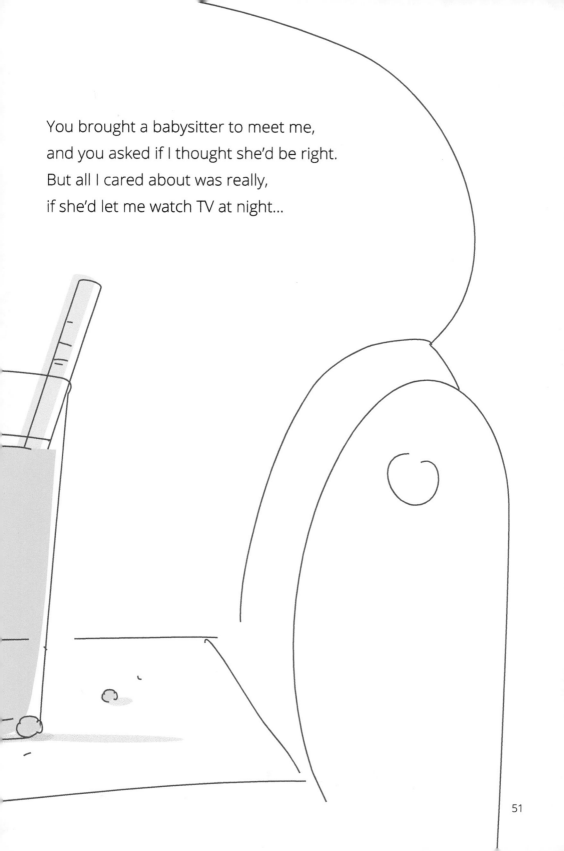

You brought a babysitter to meet me,
and you asked if I thought she'd be right.
But all I cared about was really,
if she'd let me watch TV at night...

If I'm feeling really silly,
I hide under the blanket,
so you can't see me...

You know that you're big,
when mom gets you a bed,
and folds up your crib!

My bear's just a puppet, but to me he seems real.
And I know it's real silly, because I know he can't feel.
He can't think for himself, not even one thought.
Yes. He's just a doll, but I still love him a lot!

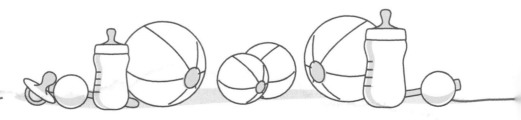

CPSIA information can be obtained
at www.ICGtesting.com
Printed in the USA
BVHW062311050719
552437BV00001B/2/P